SALM

THE BOOK THAT SPEAKS LIFE

AYUSH SHARMA

*To my parents, and a birthday gift to
my loveliest sister(s)*

♡♡♡

Contents

Preface

"Life is an untiring teacher."

Transitioning from a juvenile teen to an adult was never easy for me. I never had a big circle, but I'm thankful to every person who taught me infinite lessons about life. Taking the name of one wouldn't do justice to the other, therefore, I created the character Salm.

She is the imagery of every good and bad person who taught me how to live and the most importantly how to talk with life. I could never include all of the lessons but forthrightly, there are five principles which can promise a peaceful life if followed heartily.

I'm still in the process of adapting them to my own life but this book would remind me each day to thank and express my love for every person who is important to me, just like you reading this book.

Thanks for buying!

ԹԹԹ

Prologue

*If not enjoying the process, tell me
what success is,
If not respecting boundaries, tell me
what friendship is,
If not appreciating imperfections, tell
me what mortal is,
If not accepting more than expecting,
tell me what wisdom is,
If not responding than reacting, tell me
what peace is!*

ᗽᗽᗽ

1

Starting is always tough

And that was it...another rejection...another failure. The angst was killing me. I always took being a loner as a compliment for me. But this time it wasn't solitude but the emptiness and hollowness coming from being left lonely in my toughest times. I wish I could go to my parents and say that I'm done with my life; I can maybe hug them and say I failed this interview as well.

When I was a kid, my father used to say, "You don't have to worry, you've got my back." But this "back" seemed to be getting really old now. I remember casually talking to the only friend I made in college, "You see these people here, once we pass out nothing is gonna be the same. You, me and these all, we fools would be kicked by life to go and run. Quite possibly we even won't be together."

You know what she said, or what my parents say, "Whenever you feel like life is giving you tough questions, just talk!" My wisdom never understood whom I should talk with. And that's when something happened.

So, dramatically I went to the tallest building in my city and climbed to the top floor and screamed...!!?

Of course not, I sat on the creaking sofa on my balcony; it already had taken the shape of my butt, well metaphorically this was my entire social life.

I started ranting about my life, for 10 minutes…15 minutes, and more; the rant never seemed to stop. But then I heard a honeyed voice coming from the top of my head, "Are you done?"

I laughed thinking, "It certainly has to be life, talking to me!" and looked up; it was a soothing face looking at me with an oxymoronic angry face.

Is she talking to me? Maybe I should go and talk to her, or not? I never find people enough luring to go and talk with but today it felt like making an exception this time, (either way, I had no one to talk with) Looking up at the sky, I blew the air out of me like candles. I went to ask her.

Oh, people can get obnoxious sometimes, and so was me. Throughout my life, I never had this sense to appreciate people for the efforts they make in their relationships. Maybe I was too absorbed in the fundamentals of a Functional Friend, the friend who just stays there until you need to get a job done.

She asked me, "What made you torture your organ of speech?"

No, it is not good to open up to strangers but I started beefing up. "I've got shit to figure out, and I don't even want to do this "building block" job. I wanted to be in IT sector or possibly an enterpreneur, not a construction worker. I…" Before I could jump again into the train of the rant, she stopped me and said,

"Mind a coffee?" Deja Vu shivered through my body.

It was the last day of my college when the only friend I had, asked me the same question, and all I did was stroll away coldly. We never talked after that day; Alas! I always regret losing a friend over coffee.

But today the option was right in front of me...and that night we talked endlessly for hours without sleep.

Coffee after coffee, we sipped it like a drug. That was our first of the conversations; when two intellectual minds meet, they're sure to resonate. Echoes of ideas then produced out are enough to glorify every social circle let alone two of us.

"Who are you? I haven't seen you here before?", she switched the cup of coffee in her hands and blowing the October winds on it, said, "I'm Salm, your conscience. *Here to teach you how to talk to life.*"

For a moment I thought my soul would come out chortling at her phrase, but probably coffee can actually make someone drunk.

"So tell me why do you hate your profession as an architect? Isn't it amusing that just how block by block an architecture constructs a building, we humans do the same for relations and our lives?"

I was speechless, waiting for a convincing answer to come to me. Sometimes we just connect with people in a blink; I was really intrigued by her approach and wanted to explore this notion more, it felt like she knew a lot maybe about life as well.

So, taking down the lane of professions, we rediscovered many wild ideas which can outshine anyone's career irrespective of the field; but I was sceptical because it all seemed to be concise in the weird imaginations of our brains.

Though we talked a lot about careers and aspirations in our scholarly discussion but never seemed to agree completely. Not because we didn't have any common grounds but because there was always an addition to the argument.

"I will tell you a story, that maybe an answer to your dissatisfaction with your profession." Salm stated making herself comfortable on the sofa adjacent to me.

"A guy used to make living by selling fruits along with his ageing father in a very odd-looking cart. The son always seemed disinterested, just like you...(chuckles).

In a fuming rage, he went up to his dad and blurted, "Do you think that selling fruits can make me any better in life? I want to work for a greater vision, a greater cause."

The old man smirked, "Son, tell me if you get 100% clarity on your vision, do you think your vision is sufficient enough to get you to the cause you want to?" And the son, just like you was too much of a naive learner."

"Hey! That's an offense", inner me screamed sarcastically.

"Oh is that so!? Tell me what the son would have said." She interrogated me with a conviction.

"No, definitely not. I need execution to achieve what I want from life," the son said with a facade of ignorance.

The old man got interested now, "Okay, consider you got the ability for 100% execution of whatever your vision is, would that be enough?"

The son gave a thought and said, "Well, no until I put 100% hard work in whatever job I do..." the son stopped immediately and retrospected on what his father just taught him."

I could feel the lad's thoughts, *"Hardwork powers visions and without having efficeincy in that skill, the hardwork is also of no use."*

Salm interrupted me and stated, "The story isn't complete "sir"."

"The old was laughing on his child's foolishness and said, "Out of these four aspects, tell me what actually seems 100%

achievable?

The son's shoulder fell down with defeat, but he had a sense of the charm of learning a lifelong lesson from his father. Hard work is the only thing that can be mastered..."

While I was just on the edge to hear more of it, Salm stopped me saying, "This was enough for the story, you'll learn more when you're ready."

I swear that pissed me off but that's what you get when you're with Salm, a sweet disappointment.

Stories like such shape the narrative of personal identity. For me having failed in certainly everything I tried, took a heavy toll on my confidence level. Outside the parameters of my fluid identity, everyone recognized me as a confident chill guy; unfortunately, this "chillness" came from a lack of urge to expect a result.

When we fail in situations where we positively expected success, it hurts. But the resentment can cause us to not view the solution and keep looking at the problem.

"I have my own reasons for this." That's how I used to delegate every question asked by Salm concerning my inferiority complex.

"You stay in denial" she observed, I can't agree more. I stay in denial, but the fact of the matter is there ain't no more questions now, nor the long baffling conversations around wild ideas.

My father used to say, *"Nothing but your work will stay with you."* Friendships are like entities kept along the shore of the sea, meant to be washed away with upcoming waves of life. Only a stubborn person would stand there holding onto nothing but slippery sand.

Though it sounds bleak, my life has been everything but not tragic.

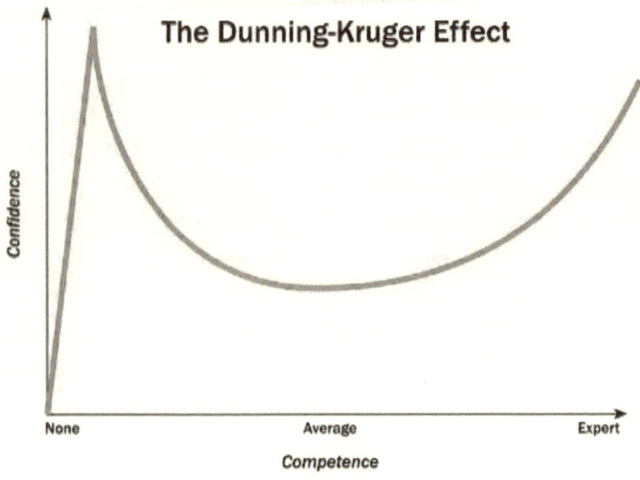

Timeline of how we interact with our reality.

This curve, though made originally to show confidence and knowledge relation, is clearly applicable to life and my relationship with it as well.

But that's not the only applicability of this graph, I remember talking about this with Salm, "Can you see how it teaches us a great thing about skills?"

"What?", her expression clearly stated she already knew it but wanted to listen to how I interpreted it.

"Just like the curve, when we start learning a skill initially, we start getting drastic noticeable results; over the period the curve starts flattening, same does our learning. This period is about excellence, about matering the nuances of the skill." With my dire attention, I presented it to Salm.

She said with a mischievous smirk, "I can see a pattern...", pausing to formulate her thoughts she said,

"When I was learning music, the first few days I could see myself getting extremely fond of hitting those notes on the guitar which in no way were perfect, still there was a sense of satisfaction. Now when I look back at those recordings, I see nothing but crap unrhythmic notes."

"You own a guitar!? I used to play the flute and thought that maybe I could master it in a day only but I got a reality check." I said with a sparkle in my eyes.

Well, it didn't last for long when she ended the conversation in dismay, "Yeah! You seem to be floating between extremes of being too wise but failing to use your own lessons."

With an affirmative tone, she gave an eye opener, "No skill is learnt overnight. It's like filling a pot with 10,000 drops of hours of hard work."

With these words, she left me thinking in the midnight breeze. I was again sitting there in the darkness, and probably for the first in my life expecting to see someone again. Her words had left a short-lived impact on me for sure.

The foundations of the building are laid

ᐅᐅᐅ

I don't appreciate people often but Salm is a genius for sure; another day it took me 10 minutes of speech to explain something which she just summed up in a couple of words.

I had retrospectively come across a vague thought, "When we fail in the situations where we had certainly expected success, it hurts. But the resent can only cause you to not view the solution and rather keep looking at the problem."

"Is that so simple?" Salm asked.

"Maybe not, but is there any point in complaining?" I never understood this idea of complaining about our problems, and I have been a culprit too.

Complaining shows your helplessness in the situation, and the dependency to expect answers from the external world.

"People complain about the corrupt system and all, but most protests occur due to some sort of dependency on the government. If you're dependent on none, your chances of getting miserable decreases spontaneously." I stated the fact to Salm with firm belief and she looked upon it in affirmation.

But then the first sign of disagreement came, "Doesn't that sound like cliché though?"

"I see no bad in that, to get in the top 1% you have to do what 99% others are not doing, that's a cliché too..." I uttered with an aggressive tone, maybe I was not so used to abrupt disagreement with the beliefs I had solidified over years.

That was the beauty of Salm, her awareness of life, I would barter every possession of mine for this level of wisdom.

"I feel it should be tweaked to do what you yourself 99% of the time isn't doing. Invest your day in skill building, testing would be the job of the world. Ayush, if you'll keep looking towards the world's 99% that would turn you maniac. Instead focus on smaller habits that you can cultivate."

This line holds great importance to me for two reasons;

one, change of perspective;

two, now call me mad or what that's the third time in total she called me by name since the day we met.

Salm used to say, "Formidable for the world but not for me." That was her confidence without bothering about the details of it; I think too much about minuscule things. She always called me an overthinker because of that. Such small details like calling me by name, appreciating me and showing care in small instances just makes me excited.

"*A person's name is to him or her the sweetest and most important sound in any language.*" – Dale Carnegie.

So does to me;

But what is more intriguing, is the idea of forming small habits. This idea has changed my life more than anything. At any time, life gets hard on us, we can always go back to the values our parents cultivated in us.

Salm just touched my heart with these lines, "*Until we have parents as our backbone, we shouldn't seek anything but them.*" They can be wrong sometimes but not the values they try to teach us. Lessons of moral science only get old when we try to bring rationality everywhere.

We both came to an instant agreement, "One of the reasons we're still surviving in this vague world is because of the strong foundations our parents laid for us." I guess me and Salm was lucky in this aspect, not everyone is.

Found the right amount of material for construction

ppp

In the afternoon, I decided to take a small nap to compensate for the hardships of my job. Just then I thought of a fad people preach, "How to stay motivated?"

A satisfactory answer, in that case, would be, "Hardships and Pain itself makes the path for motivation." I discussed this idea with Salm; without pretending to get it in the first instance she asked, "Is that some kind of bluff you sermonise, Mr. Rational Monk?"

Well, can't deny she has a good sense of humour.

"When I talk about pain and hardships, there is a four-year phase of strenuous hard work in each one's life. In India it starts mostly with JEE and the first two college years. If the train is left then the next one would be tough to climb. Just like trends are left unattended." While just saying this I realised exactly why my life was tough.

Salm deliberately brought this question to my consciousness, and the way revelation occurred blew my mind. I never gave myself enough back to life during that phase, and now life is extracting it with force.

This was not enough that Salm came with another intricacy, "But why so much hassle in the search of illusionary perfection? You don't have to be the best in the rest. *Just be so mediocre that you know what it means to be the best and failure both at the same time.*"

The grace with which she knocked me out of this conversation was smooth. How can a person not admire someone who can bring this much clarity to vague and abstractness?

Her words of wisdom were not yet over, "You talked about JEE right, why do you think parents act so forcibly to push us into this race?"

"I know that well, it's not that they deliberately force us on certain things. It's just the standardisation in our society. Parents do not consider our skill levels enough to give them confidence that we can do something good out of that career. Therefore, the only standards left for them is our academia and thus 99% of pupils are pushed into that."

"Exactly dude! Education was never about learning new things; it is the training of the mind to learn. That's what schools focus on, building the muscle of mind to learn through life."

I feel I really got her idea very well, "That means instead of shitting around what schools and coaching institutes are giving in the name of education, we should focus on interaction of our behavioural patterns and our memory with the reality; that how we would react to life, which implies the only possible way to get success in the exactness is..."

The ideas took pace, our thoughts started syncing, and with unison in the voice, the conversation came up to just a verse –

Get so good at a skill that you're undeniable.

Success can never be measured as it is just a form of greed; what you can measure is the difference in levels of your skills.

Salm says, "Well in this competition driven world the only we can build ourselves is if we have skills better than almost all."

"That would be truly getting into the top 1%. Get yourself so better that the rejection starts feeling underrated for you."

That was just an average conversation with Salm that ended with a banger.

The building seems to grow up.

ﭏﭏﭏ

2

Sharing is caring

"Have you ever read about bonds in chemistry?" I asked Salm.

"Yeah! must have, I don't remember much though." She giggled.

"In covalent bonds there's a mutual sharing of electrons which leads to the strongest bonds. In the case of a coordinate bond, it's from one end only, thus the bond strength is also weak…" Salm interrupted me and said, "Guess what! You're gonna say next, this implies relations as well."

I get so happy when she would complete my sentences because that gives me a sense of belongingness. Humans have a fundamental need to share their reality with others. It comes due to the fact of social validation and approval.

In the touch of credence I said, "If one of the friends, or parteners isn't as much as dedicated the connection would be static; vice versa the connection between two equivalent personalities adds balance to the relation."

Salm added, "Oh! That's not really true though, but yeah. You seem to be acting like a sage but hear me, success in professional life doesn't mean you're getting good at relations as well. *After all life isn't just about forming blocks but revisiting them time to time to check their condition."*

Oh, dear! That just felt like she was hinting at me to talk to all of the people whom I have been ignoring for a long time.

Saying to my parents that I love them.....Having a conversation with my sister on her favourite topic...Checking up on my old college friends.

"These tasks feel minuscule but add a great depth to any sort of relationship. You cultivate habits to get memories, the better the intent the positive the impressions. The way you'll talk to me, response would be contemplated." And that was the day when I got a subtle sign that Salm was actually "me".

She was teaching me just like an elder and wise saint, how to talk to life. Dramatically it would have been a super magical revelation but to me, it just happened while sitting on my butt-shaped sofa.

This small affirmation made me mad for my life, because if Salm is the manifestation of my conscience, then that was the best thing happening to me. I believed in my life, my Salm again.

One might think I sound obsessed with this whole analogy, well that's quite sceptical to say. But still, it felt like I reached stage 2 of our friendship – When intellectual conversations take the form of emotions. Unfortunately, this too means minute signs of "Limerence".

I remember talking day and night about her; even when the conversations were seldom, I had her in my sleep. Perhaps I was being too clingy to Salm; trying to know every small nuance of life; it was due to my impatient and faulty brain. I acquired this idea that she would caress me just like a small child and solve all my problems; in short, I was craving attention.

The situation seemed so broken because, of course, our relationship didn't have a framework to fit in. Romantic Partners? Nah! That's gross; Well then friends? Too weak a connection considering the amount I was obsessed with her imagery. Salm simply said, *"The more you define your relationship with someone, more is the possibility of despair."* There are times when we could do nothing but remorse for the perplexity of human relationships.

I have to admit with this sort of fondness you're bound to have problems, some of them might be too serious. But I don't think there is anything wrong with this need to belong with someone. I had a lot in my journal to say to Salm, but it never felt like doing so; either way, I know her well enough to know that she already knows my emotions.

That's when she came up with another interesting story.

"So this one would be more relatable to the younger ones. A boy was a great friend to a girl, they would spend hours daily talking to each other about the world and their lives. They both weren't couples but had a good bond, at least that's what the guy thought. He would act nice to her without accepting anything in return.

Soon the girl started feeling uneasy about the same; she feared the boy would end up losing himself just for the sake of her friendship. She wasn't very good at feeling connections but cared for that boy.

One day she said to him, "You know, we can't be friends anymore. In the long term, our friendship would just cause you harm. To be a friend to me, you need not lose your own identity."

Salm looked into my eyes and said, "The girl was right...but so was the guy who said-

"But rather than just breaking ties we could sit and talk about the ways to amend it. You're important to me and just

mere this thought gives me more harm than our friendship would."

I remember studying a concept of shared reality, which just fitted right in this story, "Everyone has his own identity which he wishes to share with others, that small portion is shared among them. In a relationship too, the amount of shared reality sometimes defines how good your relationship is going to be. But the problem begins when we start killing our own reality to be a part of theirs."

"But don't you think that the functioning and wiring of the mind makes us realise that there can only be some degree of shared experience with someone. You and me looking at the same object can have an abstract idea as the same but on a deeper level it is a different experience for both of us."

Salm rhetorically said, "There's a place maybe that you love but I would hate that same due to a personal experience. And any day, you should keep your personal narrative ahead of anyone, even me. Everyone seems to be searching for something to give a meaning, but at the end only we can give it a meaning"

She was right in saying that maybe very blunt too, because every time I got reminded that she is nothing but my mind speaking to me, it pricked my heart like a needle. My field of view had been narrowed to not see the wider picture.

Salm added, "You know in human relations, there is no good and bad person, we just become authors of our worlds and start treating the other person as a villain. Instead of complaining about not getting enough recognition for your efforts in relations or wanting to be loved, start leaning towards sharing your love. Share, do not extract."

Beliefs Under Construction

ᠵᠵᠵ

One night the coffee talks came again; after a heavy day at work, all I could think about was how helpless life can make us. My whole body had been aching out from strenuous work and that's when an unpleasant conversation began between me and Salm.

"Salm I trust you for saying you ain't real, but do you trust me?" I said with a doubting eye.

"Why do you have to ask me such questions? Is it necessary to put that much emphasis on just trusting? Do you have any idea, people can't really form their minds for things, it's just a bias which can help them in coming to a conclusion." She had a great angry look on her face, because yeah,

Life responds to the way you talk!

"You're right!", and she was; this was rude behaviour but practical. I too clearly don't rely upon anyone because that's not how this world is. You can ask someone to walk along with you on the dead road but only you can reach your grave.

That's just so much truth about life, "Nothing's gonna eventually stay with you, 5 years more and we will be in the rat race to get jobs and get married. The beauty of life too, comes in the change; anxiety ensues when you resist that change."

The best way to form friends I think is, at least when it comes to academics – Performative Friends.

I talked about this with Salm, "Don't you think it is too much asking from one person to be everything and friend?"

"Well yeah maybe, after all friendship is all about sharing common experience or maybe reality. I can't guarantee to always have a good day and if there's co-dependency and not interdependency, both of them are meant to suffer. If you would start fixating on the end result of a relationship, it would never sustain and eventually die leaving miseries for both."

"You mentioned codependency, well that's what your story was about, right? Often people negotiate their identity for the other person's opinions (seen mostly in the case of men). There's a high chance of you breaking down with guilt and anxiety if the fights or negotiations between you both are always won by one person. Maybe overexpression is the cause of that..."

Salm is the perfect person for such conversations because then you don't have to think before speaking; there are no formalities involved just straight emotions, "Just keep your Personal Narrative ahead of any relation, on any given day. Clinginess will kill both of you. If you assume that changing yourself or losing your identity for another person is worth it, then just think of a possibility that maybe the person is in relation with you due to that reality but if you just loose that then it would have consequences."

I roared with a sense of enlightenment, "That's exactly what G.H. Mead said- *Not only do individuals shape their self-concepts according to the perspectives of others, but also that people's views of themselves are continually maintained according to these adopted ideas.*"

"I mean no one understands, *you can be completely different from your friend and still be friends.*" Salm and I too can be taken into account in this case. We have a lot of common things but still, our realities are not aligned, but still, we respect each other's boundaries.

At the end of the day, "Humans are weird (Shwetabh Gangwar), everyone has their own problems existing outside the domain of friendships and relations. Solipsism, a philosophical idea that only one's mind is sure to exist; knowledge of anything outside one's own mind is unsure; the external world and other minds cannot be known and might not exist outside the mind. Therefore, all others' behaviour is contingent with your experience." I referred this to Salm.

"Perhaps then the ideal advice for relations is..." again our thoughts caught the rhythm and synced to say-

Set clear boundaries about how much reality you both share.

"That's what a performative friend is; call me selfish or what but you should be clear cut that what is the purpose of you agreeing to share reality with a person", and that's what life speaks.

I later brought up a not-so-pleasant question which has been bothering me, "You're continuously speaking about making friends, shared reality, is that even necessary? Is that what life is speaking to you?"

With a small pause, I continued, "I really like this concept for those who are willing to make friends, but for a random person, let's suppose who has surpassed, better messed up every friendship, this seems like jumping from a cliff. Why should I make an effort again?"

To be very honest, this hurt me a lot. I would make efforts only to be ghosted by people; whenever I started feeling like having a person whom I can trust even an iota, I hold that relation so tightly that eventually chokes out, maybe I was too involved in my own thinking to ignore my impact on surroundings and people.

"You're right! No matter how much my mind is in denial, friendship is always a two-way process. Whereas I don't think it is necessary but...we all project ourselves on others, and these intricate relations help us in understanding, if not the other person, ourselves better."

With a heavy heart, I just rose from the discussion table, I felt the burden of all my relations coming upon me within the blink of an eye. My eyes were quite moist and grave to react in any way, and no amount of coffee stopped me from sleeping that night with the wild memories running inside my head.

Finding the symmetry and balance in the building

ᐯᐯᐯ

3

Imperfection: The mother of perfection

———◆♡◆———

"It's okay to be shit and reckless!"

At first glance, Salm seems to be a complex character, like every other human, dunno why people don't understand this fact; if a person shows the intent to understand the other person, they can tone down the complex layers too.

I remember once I got really low about a particular failure related to my career, basically, I was just pushing myself too hard for perfectionism.

Before I started listening to the true nature of life, it felt like life was yelling at me, "This is how your life should be." And so, all I did was try to mimic the sublimity of an ideal lifestyle.

Salm can pursue a good career as a life coach if she had half the seriousness of life as me. Too contrasting here we're, I am an overthinker and she? She is grown, period.

"This isn't only impossible and exhausting to pursue; it's also unnatural to aim for nothing less than perfection." Salm said.

Yes, I remember talking with her about how we should go about mastering a skill, but mastering seems far more plausible than achieving perfection. I quoted Taleb to her, "Life is much, much easier when you treat all humans as flawed and imperfect, but flawed in quite different ways."

I always wanted to make everything best if not perfect, the fights between me and Salm were just a by-product of this.

"*Not all conflicts have immediate solutions.*" That's what Salm said to me when I narrated to her an incident from my past,

"I need a break! Break from everything, break from you!" My best friend left me alone in happenstance when I was already in the darkest hour of my life. Never could I look into those eyes again which had hatred and anger for me rather than love.

I was just in my building looking at the marbles getting placed on the floor. They were dull and pale yet, we knew that for sure later on, we can clean every stain and the shine would return soon. "Is it the same with relations? Can we really amend any conflict?"

"We can, but nobody does. Most of the time the severity of fights just eliminates any sort of connection left between them, and nobody wants to be hurt the second time. Time then eventually heals every wound, but not relations."

There was a moment of awkward silence between both of us and then Salm said, "How good is your memory?"

I can't deny, boasting my memory makes me feel special just for a while; I am very good at names provided I get a small backstory of the person.

She smirked, "So that you claim to have a decent memory, it's time to finish the old man's story for you."

"The old man looked towards his cart, which was nothing less than a crap assembled. With an affirmative look he narrated to his son, "When I was your age, I lost my father and mine house as well. I didn't have any skills or any vision but still, I decided to make friends with hard work. I used to keep vegetables in the kurta my father gave me before dying. While selling the vegetables, I collected junk waste that could come in handy to me someday."

He sighed a bit and grieved, "Day after Day with imperfections, I build a perfect cart; the cart which kept me alive so far. I am not saying you to keep it as ancestral good. Learn this, my son, every flawless-looking thing is just an impression of perfection built after years and years of imperfections."

Salm spoke softly, "Relationships, people, careers and most importantly life, they can never be perfect. Conflicts are bound to happen, things are obliged to end. Soon my presence too."

This wasn't something I was hearing the first time though; a certain truth about life is everything has a timeline and therefore an end. This one was a greater setback because it's hard to not be your own friend. Yeah, Salm is nothing but a deep-rooted subconscious mind talking to me at all moments. This harshness left me dumbstruck and grounded for a while.

A cup of coffee and the flooring is done

ᚦᚦᚦ

Today seems like a good day at work, maybe I have started enjoying my life...A good day at work and an evening conversation with Salm, all seems fine.

That's when I slipped from the second floor of the building to the fence...I broke my arm, and the work which I somehow had started enjoying stopped again, putting an end to my zeal abruptly.

I was damn careless and didn't see the precaution that the floor was wet. Precautions are something we all ignore just like red flags. For me, it was always ignoring the fact that I am not a demigod to do everything perfectly, nor is Salm then. She can only guide me to a better life but not an easy life.

I thought I apparently was limping so maybe I can have some time off to reflect on my life and learn more from Salm about myself. Well...

"You're on your own, kid", she faded in the air never to be seen again. I waved my hands into the wind, to see nothing but darkness all around.

How subtly she came when I needed her the most, that finesse was her departure.

I had two cups of hot coffee staring at me as if they were waiting for my company to come today again. Salm left without an explanation but here too, precautions weren't of any use; I kept ignoring her when she said, "I am here only for a while, you need to learn on your own how to celebrate your life."

For a while...for a while, I thought she was just trying to fool me...*for a while*, I thought perhaps she was gonna go on a hiatus...*for a while*, I finally missed a person that dearly which happens to be me.

I didn't have a speck of energy to look around, that night I just sat staring at the cups of coffee slowly turning cold. My vision was almost blurry with the tears just sitting on the edge of my eyelashes. Time kept passing away adding more numbness to my sour and injured leg. I was now crippled both physically and mentally. Out of my anxious anger, I gave a lot of shit out to Salm and my life.

It felt like a stack of problems piling up and up, over and over....maybe until I give up. But that was the only quality I had, perseverance. It was harsh, maybe necessary as a wake-up call to me.

Sometimes harshness can apparently make us realise our imperfections. Facing a separation from my counterpart made me realise a few things, "*Relationships just like humans aren't perfect in any sense. We spend fortunes tweaking ourselves, our lives, and our environment and then flood social media with pictures and videos to show the world the exquisiteness of our lives. Perfection is what we need to accomplish: a perfectly symmetrical face, a perfectly sculpted body, perfect hair, skin, jawline, house, friends, family, partner, children, vacations, or in short: an existence without fault.*"

I felt awful when Salm reacted to me in that way; I had always imagined her to be an image of perfection that I could never be. Alas! This aspiration of perfection adds nothing to our life but rather ruins the randomness of nature.

I had to apologise for my doings and the way I was acting out. Not just to Salm but to my parents, and the only friend I had.

This event made me realise the importance of a good friend. She stopped me from feeling bad about myself. I was harsh on people and so ultimately life did the same to me.

She once sarcastically quoted in the tone of a scholar, "We worship perfection because we can't have it; if we had it, we would reject it. Perfect is inhuman, because humanity is imperfect" (Yeah, I realised later this was just a quote by Fernando Pessoa.)

Construction is @Halt

ךךך

Salm was gone but not her ingenious words and some of her remarks still live rent-free in my heart and soul. Never in my senses, could I think of hurting my conscience, but yeah, I did that running for mythical perfection.

All of my wraths came out for life; why only I have to take the heat? Is it even necessary to only learn after being broken? Perhaps that was the way of life teaching us. But I have learnt how to speak to life.

I once asked Salm how life is going, and she said, "Life is exactly how it's always been and is supposed to be: generally awful and chaotic, punctuated by occasional bouts of utter catastrophe, and relieved by rare moments of relative happiness and contentment — and this from an optimist..."

This is what life speaks to me now, every time I end up disappointed with people or in particular my life itself-

Appreciate and embrace the imperfections

We can't appreciate Fridays without having to experience a Monday. Fights would happen, and people would come and go, but Salm's words got tattooed in my soul.

Now having the dust settled it was time to reflect upon whatever I said to Salm in the rush of anger. That's where life again comes in and helps me.

ᗡᗡᗡ

4

Accepting more than expecting

Fights are often exhausting; people speak ill of each other and sometimes the harshest truths are said in those intense moments only.

"Hurtful yet the words may have the potential to reveal what a person truly thinks of you." I read this somewhere, and almost had this opinion coded in my mind but Salm brought up a new perspective on it.

"When we engage in a fight, we deliberately say stuff to hurt the person, and if you start believing that to be true, it is nothing but a fallacy. We, humans, are so expert at lying or forming momentary emotions; considering my words to be an ultimatum is nothing but foolishness." As blunt as a knife, Salm said that.

Maybe I have to agree with that, "When we have a fight with our parents, there can be some hurtful words too but eventually we know that they would love us anyhow. Similarly, if you understand a person, you can easily distinguish when they're just acting out of rage."

One of my favourite stoic quotes is "If a person speaks ill of you, it's either true or false. If it's true, then you should accept it as who you are. If it's false, then accept them as foolish, and their opinion can be disregarded."

We think that maybe holding hard onto people will change them the way we want to but that never happens in the real world. Friendships, family and relationships are all about freedom, the freedom of expressing your noblest form to the person.

Salm and I really used to have existential conversations after our fights. Now it feels like life has started acting nicer to me; even if not wiser I'm knowing how life speaks.

That makes me realise, "Negativity/ Fights aren't always bad. One often thinks that accepting the negative situation leads to a negative life. But in fact, it is quite the opposite. You cannot see the whole without accepting the negative, and living a fulfilling life is about living through wholeness. There's this realization I got that acceptance brings you closer to the truth."

"Till where though? I personally think that keeping expectations is healthy because that's the sign of growth." Salm glanced over this thought.

"Yes, expecting a little is healthy but when we start forming foundations of our lives based on expectations, life gets miserable. Nature's default position is change. As everything is born from it and nothing is static; and because nothing lasts, nothing is worthy of worry." Though I wish it could have been as easier than I said this but Salm understands this quite well and thus came the storytime.

"A person had a severe fight with one of his friends, and couldn't let it go; it was just damn hard. They both have been friends for 5 years and this was the roughest of the fights. Nobody was truly at the fault alone, one of them had started

dating a girl. This led the friendship to be questioned, and most people just start prioritising the relationship over others.

Soon things started falling apart, and Salm was remembered again. Over time when he managed to move on, and ultimately he didn't lose anything. Memories of his best friend always stayed with him, and mere acceptance of the incident revealed many things about his own self and his behavioural flaws."

That was an interesting insight Salm gave me, "Wow! How interesting it sounds. What I inferred is that *in the process of letting go, we will lose many things from the past, but will find ourselves."*

"Yes, they say nothing is worthy of worry, everything has a timeline. In day-to-day life, we attach to everything. Everything that makes us happy, that makes us sad, angry, depressed but eventually, all of those states will become impermanent. Just think for a second, since you woke up today, how many thoughts you had. Look closely and try to realize how each and every thought went away, either by just forgetting that thought or acting on that thought."

"Either way, you don't remember stuff!" We giggled a bit, but then there was a deafening silence to absorb the heaviness of the words said about life.

That was the time when we both could sense ourselves falling apart over time and so that one was a consoling conversation for both of us. Non-attachment is one of the hardest concepts to implement when you've been indoctrinated and conditioned so severely over the years. But without being completely nihilistic, none of these trivialities and petty worries actually matter.

In fact, most of us wouldn't desire half of what we do if we weren't constantly bombarded by social media and propaganda telling us we're not good enough, telling us we'll be happy "when" we reach or obtain something.

"When the external world doesn't give answers, you have no choice but to look within. I think realizing how impermanent the material world is makes it easier to let go." I presented a thought process that I had in my mind to Salm.

Salm reverted, "To me, the essence of life is boundless and unabashed self-expression. Instead of hoping for a life free of misfortune, it's better to wish ourselves the fortitude to handle adversity."

I remember Marcus Aurelius talking about it in his book Steps to Knowledge, *"Pain is always a decision that you make in response to any stimuli in your environment. The body will have physical pain if it is so stimulated, but that is merely a sensory response.*

It is not the true pain that hurts you. The pain that hurts you is the crown of thorns of your own ideas and assumptions, your own misgivings and misinformation and your own unforgiveness towards yourself and the world...You may feel that you have been wronged by another or by the world... This, however, is not how knowledge views you, and you must learn not to view yourself in this way... Without condemnation upon the world and upon yourself, the mind is at peace already."

While this seems a long journey but that is what life speaks to me-

Start accepting more than expecting.

And that's when I finally accepted Salm's absence; some things are just bound to happen and the best we can do is get comfortable with the ugly truths we've to face on the daily basis.

Most of the time it isn't big fights that cause separations, just like how working on the construction site we sometimes miss the nuanced flaws in the symmetry of the building, the minute conflicts cause a heavy toll on relations, and I still remember Salm's precious words, *"People aren't against you, they're for themselves."*

There isn't much left to think about. Add nothing of your own from within, and that's the end of it. Accept other people, misfortune, change and your own merry existence cause just like the seasons turning on the chart people have their personal lives to handle. Therefore, acceptance opens up a way for more possibilities of life and growth; after all, it's all about how we react and that's what life spoke to me at last.

Construction about to end

ᗡᗡᗡ

5

Respond, Do not react

So finally, the day has come, my plaster was removed and so was my problem with the problems of life. Reaching the site I could see a ready building only requiring finesse work. They were all waiting for me; in just a span of 30 minutes all the lessons Salm and life gave me, were rolling over my eyes.

My skills were unmatchable with any worker there, they waited for me to recover and give the building a final touch. My hard work, my perseverance, and my skills saved my job and earned me respect.

Spending time to amend relations and showing gratitude to my colleagues not just improved their behaviour towards me, but made me more confident about my own self. I wasn't very much of a reader but Salm told me about a famous quote from Charles Horton Cooley, "*I am not who you think I am; I am not who I think I am; I am who I think you think I am.*"

I don't know in what way others interpret it, but for me, it means that identity is a social construct and you need good people to help you feel good about yourself; you can not really do anything when situations are not favourable.

I missed Salm's motherly support who taught me how beautiful it is to accept hardships and flaws of our identity and self. We neither need perfect people nor relations, all we need is acceptance. Most importantly there's a cost to everything. A hand can't hold more than one cup of coffee.

Flaws can be fixed, but blunders can't

ﭖﭖﭖ

Ludwig Wittgenstein had an entire miserable life, which is depicted well in his writings. But the day he died his words were, "Tell them I've had a wonderful life."

My life never got easy, in fact, things went on quite a downfall after this project. Most of us do not want an exhausting life, and the same for our relationships; we want them to be simple, but when the sun isn't on our horizon, we have two options. We can either create a fuss out of unpleasant situations by using penetrative words to feed our anger or maybe we can just respond rather than react.

Salm and I don't talk, but still, I know that any day she would counter-argue on the above words, "Sometimes maybe you can just not think about whether you're reacting or responding, cause you need to be at least noble and honest to yourself when such situations occur."

And then I would say, "But if we neglect these things, and focus on what's not in our control, we are in a position of weakness. Especially when we cling to what's not up to us, we set ourselves up for a life of suffering. After all, we cling to a lot things – people, objects, situations and thoughts too."

I just had an insight from my life which happens to Stoic philosophy as well- *Duress under Stress.* It means adapting like a streamlined flow of the river which doesn't resist the obstacles, just lets them come and go. There may be a lot of chaos outside but just being centred on the inside makes you stand tall and wise in tougher times.

While gazing at the sun setting low, I added, "Well to be honest, we think the things we cling to, are somewhere a necessity of our lives; but the more we shed the things which aren't ours, we'll reach to the point where nothing except us remains. The minimum thing that is required for survival is – I."

"Isn't it this dichotomy of control?" Salm would have definitely interrogated me; I would have laughed and used another interesting analogy for the same.

Often, I used to tease Salm for sometimes getting angry with my child-like habits, "Be like a water bottle, not a soda bruh!" She would just glance over my sarcastic smile continuing to show her anger. Yeah, this is how imaginations run in my head; that's how I understand the abstract definitions which I otherwise never could.

> "*Love for me is a season of gratitude, care and compassion with stakes practical yet high,*
> *Friendship for me is the season of freedom, joy and dedication but I got none, sigh.*
> *Relationship is the season I never understand, it is gonna be a learning phase,*
> *Life? It is fun, atleast that's the lie we buy.*"

I responded to Salm's question with a pinch of analogy, "Temptation to remove lemon from the water is sheer waste of time. Yeah, you were right! Epictetus explored this dichotomy of control in his writings. Some things are in our control, others not. If we manage to concern ourselves with the things in our control, we are in a position of strength. Our dependency on anything adds up weaknesses for us."

Salm surely corrected this bold statement though, "But having weaknesses doesn't mean we're weak actually, we're social beings and having people around us is good for our mental and physical health. But I get your point, we really need to be cautious about what sort of people we are surrounded with. Our very sense of wellbeing is at gunpoint when we cling to the fickle, unreliable outside world. The reason I do not feel attached to anyone, not even you; and the reality is unfortunate but that's how I've become socially."

"You must have a strong resilience to say that on my face. Well, worry is a terrible waste of imagination. So I'm gonna let it absorb patiently. I always knew we can never be good pair but still we both will exist to care for each other, and that's more than enough for me."

I like things to end on a good note and of course a cup of coffee, but with Salm it was sudden. The coffee which I denied in my college was balanced.

I remember many Buddhists saying this, "Suffering comes from desire; pain is inevitable, suffering for the same is option." That's how me and Salm, aka, my conscience, and my attachment to this world fell apart.

Life parted ways with me saying –

We can't control how things happen but we can control our response to them.

Any day a cliché line, but let me remind you what Salm said about clichés, "Just because we can't appreciate enough of the common tropes/habits taught by our parents and elders possibly, we remain in denial of the same."

I understand what life says to me but sometimes I just give up on it and let myself feel the moment, and the emotion. Salm just said one thing to me, *"If you gave yourself even a fraction of the encouragement you give others, imagine how far you could get."*

We all need this attitude to start taking responsibility for ourselves. Friends come, they share a bond, things fall apart...and the cycle continues. I've realized deeply that all I got is me, and so it shouldn't be the responsibility of anyone else to make me happy. If they do it is the best to happen with a person; finding needles in the hay isn't easy.

And that was the final floor of our friendship, the building was ready. That means we do not have any more common grounds but a lot of memories and lessons. I got better at talking to life, but on the premise, the purpose of Salm was defied, and so we had to part ways. Still, I hope, we both will get back someday to renovate our building and maybe reconstruct some half-baked blocks of this magnificent building, build with emotions and memories of life, and,

Ready to live

ᗞᗞᗞ

If you managed to read this book till here know that you're gonna be doing great in your life, and here's a small token of appreciation from Salm to you.

"Hello, I'm Salm. If ever the hardships of life overpower you, consider me there to help. Maybe in the form of a friend, your parents, or someone whom you love, I will be there to cheer you up; to make you fall in love with life; to take you to the freedom to be alive to live and not just to win. Life isn't a race but a labyrinth."

Here's a summary of 5 major lessons from the book.

Get so good at a skill that you're undeniable.

Set clear boundaries about how much reality you both share.

Appreciate and embrace the imperfections

Start accepting more than expecting.

We can't control how things happen but we can control our response to them.

❧❧❧

About Me

I'm Ayush Sharma, just an ordinary guy with a lot of curiosity. This is my third book in number and is heavily inspired by my personal life. My Salm is all the friends that I was fortunate to spend time with, most of them are gone onto their separate paths already. Some are still bothered by my presence on daily basis. But even if the ending was bad or things would not on good terms, in future too, I'm still thankful for the precious time of their life they showered on me.

I don't claim to write something extraordinary, in fact, you'll find most of this information in any other book too, but I hope this book helps you to discover your Salm, and make life more fulfilling for you.

Connect with me on Instagram: **ayush_sharman** or you can mail me at **ashsharman123@gmail.com** to drop your reviews. I would love to have a conversation with you all, and you can also get a copy of my other two publications for free.

1. Horrible Sins: Recarnation of Life
2. Book of Why's & How's: Exclusively for Teenagers & Students

ᐅᐅᐅ

**Karmanye Vadhikaraste Ma Phaleshou Kada
Chana
Ma Karma Phala Hetur Bhurmatey
Sangostva Akarmani**

*"Darkness is all around, you have to find the source
of light for you"*

ᐅᐅᐅ

9 798888 339381